Delilah's Delightful Dream

RUTH LERNER PERLE

Illustrated by Deborah Colvin Borgo

GROLIER
BOOKS

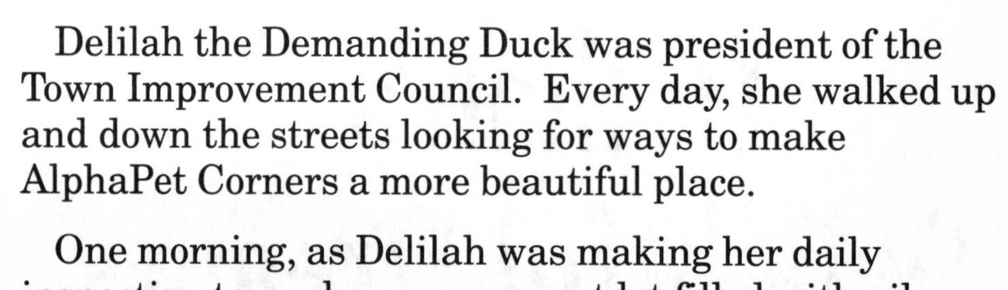

Delilah the Demanding Duck was president of the Town Improvement Council. Every day, she walked up and down the streets looking for ways to make AlphaPet Corners a more beautiful place.

One morning, as Delilah was making her daily inspection tour, she saw a vacant lot filled with piles and piles of junk.

"Oh dear, oh dear, oh dear!" cried Delilah, "just look at that dump!"

SOAP
No Dumping!

As Delilah went to inspect the lot, she tripped and fell. *Plop*! Her pencils and pads went flying, and a lamp shade landed right on her head.

"Yikes!" cried Delilah. "Just look at this place! It's dirty, dangerous and disgusting! It's a nightmare. Somebody must do something about this."

Delilah got up, ran to a house across the street and knocked on the door.

Sylvester the Stubborn Squirrel opened it.

“Hey! Sylvester!” demanded Delilah. “Get rid of all that disgusting junk across the street. It looks disgraceful. You have to do something!”

“It’s not *my* mess. I don’t have to do anything if I don’t want to!” said Sylvester.

Delilah went next door. Justin the Joking Jackal and Tina the Truthful Tiger were doing the dishes.

"Look at that mess across the street!" Delilah shouted. "You should be cleaning *that* instead of those dirty dishes!"

"Well, well, aren't you the bossy one!" answered Justin. "By the way, that hat fits you just right. You look better in the shade! Ha,ha,ha,ha!"

"The truth is, you really *are* too bossy," said Tina.

Delilah stomped from door to door shouting, “Look at this dump! It’s a nightmare! Get your brooms and hoses and clean up this mess!”

But none of the AlphaPets paid any attention to Delilah.

“No way!” cried Nelly the Naughty Newt.

“Clean up this mess! Clean up this mess! No way! No way!” repeated Monty the Mimicking Mouse.

Just then, Wendy the Wise Woodchuck came riding by on her bicycle.

"Hello, Delilah," said Wendy. "That's an interesting hat you're wearing. Reminds me of a lamp I once had."

"What's wrong with everybody?" asked Delilah, taking the lampshade off her head. "Why won't they do what I tell them?"

"Maybe it's the *way* you tell them," said Wendy. "Remember, you catch more flies with honey than with vinegar."

Delilah went back across the street and picked up her notepads. Then she sat down and thought about what Wendy said.

"Maybe Wendy's right," she said to herself. "I'll try my very best to ask them nicely. I'll do anything to clean up that dump."

Soon afterwards, Vinnie the Vocal Vulture came over to see what was happening. Delilah smiled her very best smile. She said, "Vinnie, dear, would you help me clean up this dirty, dirty dump? Think how beautiful our town would be if everything were neat and clean."

"Well, well, well," said Vinnie, stepping up on a crate. "It would be an honor and a pleasure to help you out, Ms. Delilah. And a great opportunity. Yes, a great opportunity indeed! If I've said it once, I've said it a thousand — no, a million times. That's right, a *million* times! This vacant lot should be cleaned up. And it should be cleaned up by the best and the brightest citizens of AlphaPet Corners. Gather 'round, everybody. I say, gather 'round! Are you all with me?"

"Yes, yes!" the AlphaPets shouted.

“Let’s start right now,” cried Ivy the Impatient Iguana.

“I’ll get my dump truck,” said Rupert the Resourceful Rhinoceros.

So, everybody rolled up their sleeves and got busy.

Tina and Justin collected all the bottles and cans.

Ivy helped Rupert load his dump truck.

Sylvester and Vinnie fixed the fence.

Nelly swept the litter.

And Monty raked the leaves.

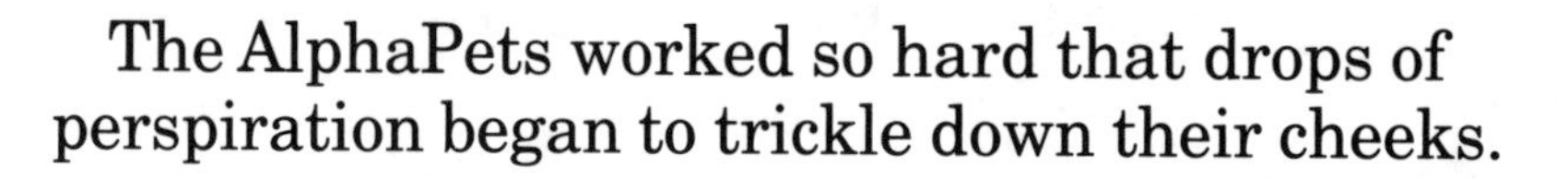

The AlphaPets worked so hard that drops of perspiration began to trickle down their cheeks.

"Hurry up! Hurry up! There's still a lot to be done!" shouted Delilah. "You're not working fast enough."

When they heard Delilah's demands, the AlphaPets stopped working.

Rupert stopped his truck. Sylvester and Vinnie put down their hammers. Nelly dropped her broom and Monty dropped his rake.

"Hey, Delilah! Don't be such a Bossy Flossie!" said Nelly. "We're doing the best we can."

"Oh! I guess I forgot," said Delilah. "I'm sorry. You're all doing a great job."

Soon the lot was all neat and clean.

Delilah looked around and said, “This looks great! Wouldn’t it be dreamy if we had a little park or playground here?”

“Hmm,” said Rupert. “I have an idea. Delilah, suppose you go home and don’t come back until we call you.”

“But..but...” sputtered Delilah. “I didn’t mean...”

“Never mind,” said Rupert. “For once, do what *we* tell *you* to do.”

As soon as Delilah left, the AlphaPets huddled around Rupert and he told them his idea.

"Bzzz, bzzz, bzzz," he whispered. "Bzzz, bzzz, bzzz."

"Hooray!" everyone shouted. "This will be fun."

So, everyone had a new job to do.

Vinnie made a tire swing and hung it from a tree.

Tina nailed a plank to a broken barrel to make a seesaw.

Nelly and Monty tied an old basket to the fence post while Sylvester and Justin arranged planks on the ground.

Rupert stacked some bricks and laid a door across them to make a table.

And Ivy planted daisies, dahlias and delphiniums.

Like magic, the empty lot became a beautiful playground.

Tina ran home to get her radio and call Delilah.

Soon, Delilah returned carrying a tray with a big white doily spread on it. It was piled high with dozens of double-dipped doughnuts and glasses of delicious cold drinks.

Delilah looked around and said, "Oh, my goodness! This is the dreamiest park in the whole wide world!"

"Now don't anyone dare make a move!" she demanded. "I insist that you all sit down while I serve these delicious delicacies."

Vinnie stood up and raised his glass. "Well, I declare!" he said with a broad smile. "Unaccustomed as I am to public speaking, I must say, I do say, I insist on saying — yes, I *insist* on saying, that that is the most delightful demand Delilah has ever delivered. Delilah has inspired us all to turn a nasty nightmare into a delectable dream. I hereby propose that we dedicate this playground to Delilah the Duck, and name this park DELILAH'S DREAM."

All the AlphaPets clapped and cheered. Then Tina turned on the music and everyone danced and danced.

While she was dancing, Delilah saw Wendy standing at the entrance of the park. Delilah ran over to her. "Don't stand there! You have to come dance, Wendy!" Delilah demanded. Then she remembered and smiled. "Er, ah, that is *please* come in and dance."

"That's a honey of an idea," said Wendy.

"A delightful idea," agreed Delilah.

You definitely must learn these delightful words with me ... *please*.

doily

door

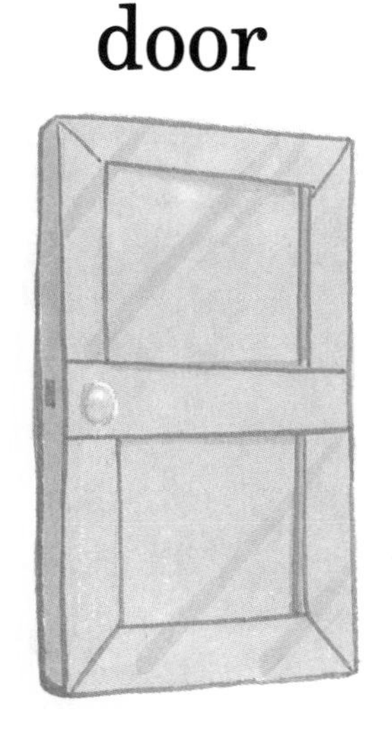

daisy

doughnut

dog

dartboard

Look back at the pictures in this book and try to find these and other things that begin with the letter D.

Aa Bb

Gg Hh

Mm Nn Oo Pp

Uu Vv Ww